Just What Mama Needs

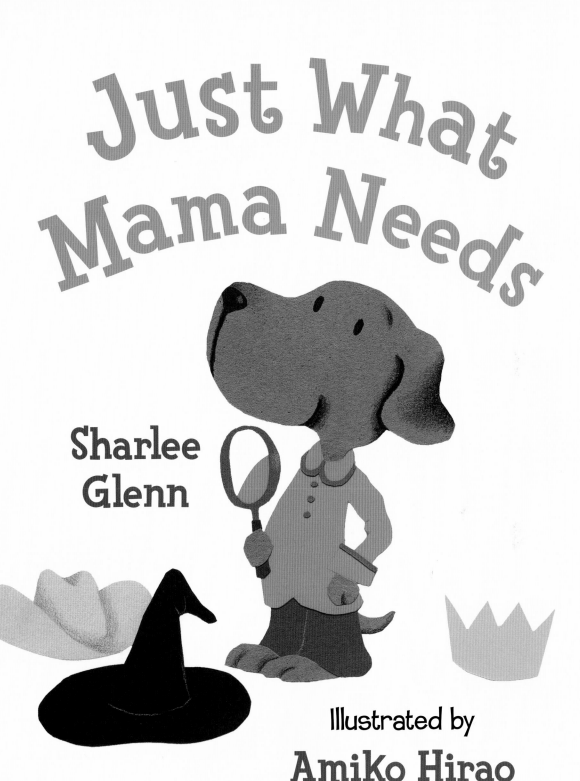

Sharlee
Glenn

Illustrated by

Amiko Hirao

Harcourt, Inc.   Orlando   Austin   New York   San Diego   London

In loving memory of my own mama,
who always knew just what was needed—S. G.

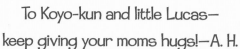

To Koyo-kun and little Lucas—
keep giving your moms hugs!—A. H.

Text copyright © 2008 by Sharlee Glenn
Illustrations copyright © 2008 by Amiko Hirao

www.HarcourtBooks.com

Library of Congress Cataloging-in-Publication Data
Glenn, Sharlee Mullins.
Just what Mama needs/Sharlee Glenn; illustrated by Amiko Hirao.
p. cm.
Summary: Abby assumes a different identity for each
day of the week until Sunday, when she is just herself.
[1. Identity—Fiction. 2. Imagination—Fiction. 3. Week—Fiction.] I. Hirao, Amiko, ill. II. Title.
PZ7.G4855Ju 2008
[E]—dc22 2005025440
ISBN 978-0-15-205759-6

First edition
A C E G H F D B

Manufactured in China

The illustrations in this book were done in collage
and colored pencil on a variety of paper surfaces.
The display type was set in Fink.
The text type was set in Coop Light.
Color separations by Bright Arts Ltd., Hong Kong
Manufactured by South China Printing Company, Ltd., China
Production supervision by Pascha Gerlinger
Designed by April Ward

On **Monday** Abby wore
a red-striped shirt, raggedy pants,
and a black patch over one eye.

She swaggered around and
sliced the air with her sword.

"Yo, ho, ho!" she shouted.

"A pirate!" said Mama. "Just what I need."
So, Abby helped Mama swab the deck.
Swish. Swish. Swash.

On **Tuesday** Abby wore
dark glasses and a big overcoat
with an upturned collar.

She peered through a magnifying glass.
"Hmm...," she said.

"I think I see a clue."

"A detective!" said Mama. "Just what I need."
So, Abby helped Mama find the missing
socks and underwear. *Aha!*

On Wednesday Abby wore
a ten-gallon hat and silver spurs.

She galloped across the prairie,
whirling her lasso in the air.

"Howdy, partner," she said,
as she reined in her horse.

"A cowgirl!" said Mama. "Just what I need."
So, Abby helped Mama round up the livestock .
Yee-haw!

On **Thursday** Abby wore a
pointy black hat and a swishy black cape.

She flew around on a broom.
"Heh, heh, heh," she cackled.

"**A witch!**" said Mama. "Just what I need."
So, Abby helped Mama mix up a delicious brew
for lunch. *Bubble. Bubble. Bubble.*

On **Friday** Abby wore poofy pants
and a towel turban on her head.

"Master, you have freed me from the magic lamp,"
she said with a deep bow. "Your wish is my command."

"**A genie!**" said Mama. "Just what I need."
So, Mama wished, and Abby:

1. made her bed
Sha-zip!

2. picked up her toys
Sha-zap!

3. put away her books
Sha-zam!

(But that's all, because
everyone knows that
with a genie, you only
get three wishes.)

On **Saturday** Abby wore a
purple robe and a golden crown.

She glided through the palace giving orders.
"Do this," she said. "Do that."

"A queen!" said Mama. "Just what I need."
So, Abby helped Mama do the royal shopping.
The store doors opened at her command.

She rode high in her silver carriage
and called out her orders:
"Five bananas! Two loaves of bread!
One jar of peanut butter!"

She helped pay with coins
from the imperial treasury.
Plink. Plink. Plink.

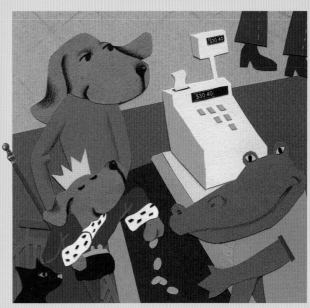

And on Sunday Abby wore
her favorite shirt.

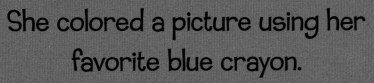

She colored a picture using her
favorite blue crayon.
She banged out "Frog Went a-Courtin'"
seventeen times on her bongo drums.

Then she lined up her stuffed
animals against the wall—tallest
to shortest—and she yodeled for them.
Yodel-o-dee-odel-o-dee-ay!

Mama came into Abby's room.
"Let's see," said Mama.
"What are you today?
An artist?"
"No," said Abby.
"A drummer?"
"No," said Abby.
"A zookeeper?
A yodeler?"
"No, and no," said Abby.
"Then what?" asked Mama.
"Today . . . ," said Abby,
"today I am . . .

"An Abby!" said Mama.
"That's what I need most of all."